Vikki
Moves To
New
Ipswich

by
Mary Ruth Weaver

AuthorHouse™
1663 Liberty Drive
Bloomington, IN 47403
www.authorhouse.com
Phone: 833-262-8899

Because of the dynamic nature of the Internet, any web addresses or links contained in this book may have changed since publication and may no longer be valid. The views expressed in this work are solely those of the author and do not necessarily reflect the views of the publisher, and the publisher hereby disclaims any responsibility for them.

Any people depicted in stock imagery provided by Getty Images are models, and such images are being used for illustrative purposes only.
Certain stock imagery © Getty Images.

This book is printed on acid-free paper.

ISBN: 978-1-6655-4148-0 (sc)
ISBN: 978-1-6655-4136-7 (hc)
ISBN: 978-1-6655-4137-4 (e)

Print information available on the last page.

Published by AuthorHouse 10/15/2021

authorHOUSE®

Dedication

I dedicate this book to my lovely daughter, Vikki Marie Gorman, with this poem I wrote for her 10th birthday.

I SAW YOU DANCING
March 14, 1984
I saw you dancing,
late last night,
when you thought no one was watching.
You twirled, and spun,
then kicked up you heels,
and gently toe stepped down the hall.
I watched from the kitchen,
around the corner from the breakfast bar.
You bent over, touched your toes
and sang a little song with high-pitched glee.
Then exited the hallway into your room.
I thought how beautiful you are,
so happy and graceful, and full of joy.
Then I smiled as tears swelled up in my eyes,
looked up and thanked God
for the joy you have given me.

Vikki

Moves To

New

Ipswich

As the sun gently crests over the horizon, we hear a yawn, a sigh, and a stretch (if one can actually hear a stretch), as Vikki awakens to a brand new day in the town of New Ipswich.

Having just recently moved to New Ipswich, Vikki hasn't quite figured out the people in the town, yet (and they're still wondering about her, too). When she asks what kind of a town is New Ipswich, everyone smiles and tells her it's just your typical little town.

Well, New Ipswich isn't exactly your typical little town, and of course, Vikki isn't exactly your typical little girl. You see, New Ipswich is a town full of love and magic. The love is from all the people who live there, and the magic is, well, it's just in the air.

Vikki, on the other hand, is a work in progress. She's a cute little girl with blonde hair, a braided ponytail on each side of her head, and a heart full of love. She has bangs that are fluffy but neat, and a turned-up little button nose that sits right on her cute little freckled face (and I do mean freckled). When people ask Vikki her name she says, "Oh, just call me plain old Vikki!" (Of course, there really isn't anything plain or old about her)

After she washes her face, she slips on her round glasses with rose-colored lenses (which is appropriate for Vikki, because that's just how she sees the world – rosy and beautiful!) Her goal in life is a modest one. She only wants to make everyone and everything happy (no matter how she has to do it)!

Vikki's day may start off like everyone else's, but let me tell you – it never quite ends up the same! On this particular day, Vikki decided, out of the goodness of her heart (for her heart truly is a good one), that she would bake a batch of cookies to take to Mrs. Pellegrino. It wasn't as if Mrs. Pellegrino needed any cookies, for you see, Mrs. Pellegrino was actually the baker's wife. But, Vikki just knew Mrs. Pellegrino would be happy to have a batch of her very own special-made cookies! This was Vikki's way of saying thank you, because The Pellegrinos had been so nice in welcoming them to New Ipswich.

Did Vikki even know how to bake cookies? Well, not exactly, but she had eaten a lot of cookies, and had visited Pellegrino's Bakery many times to sample their goodies, therefore that made her an expert on cookies – didn't it? Besides, she could bake a batch of cookies and have them delivered long before her mom and dad ever woke up!

Vikki followed the directions precisely, well, almost precisely. She may have dumped in a little too much salt, or forgotten to add the baking soda, or wasn't quite sure how to measure the brown sugar (what does 'packed' mean?). So, she added a little more of this and a little more of that, just for good measure.

Vikki wanted chocolate chip cookies, and since she loved chocolate chips, she dumped in two extra large bags. Now, to measure out the flour.

"Let's see, the recipe calls for 2 1/4 cups of flour. Does that mean two, one quarter cups? I guess so," said Vikki, so in went the two, one quarter cups of flour. (And of course, we all know that means two full cups plus one quarter of a cup, but Vikki didn't know that, so she only measured out two one quarter cups, which only equals 1/2 cup of flour).

When the cookies were done, Vikki couldn't figure out why her chocolate chip cookies didn't look quite like Mrs. Pellegrino's chocolate chip cookies. Usually the cookies were white with little bits of chocolate chips all around, but Vikki's cookies were all dark chocolate, and just a bit "fudgey-looking". (Vikki didn't know that if you didn't put enough flour in the recipe, the chocolate chips would melt into the cookie batter, making them fudge cookies, instead of chocolate chip cookies).

Well, they would do, she thought. So with the cookies done and wrapped in foil, off to Mrs. Pellegrino's she went. The kitchen? Well, that could be cleaned up later. After all, her main concern was making Mrs. Pellegrino happy!

When she was ready to go, she put on her yellow rain boots, her yellow rain coat, and her yellow rain hat. (Was it raining outside? Not yet, but Vikki just knew it would!)

She skipped along to Pellegrino's Bakery, picking up leaves and admiring their beautiful colors. Some of them she stuffed into her pockets, so that she could add them to her leaf collection later.

As Vikki came walking into the bakery, she closed her eyes and sniffed the delicious aroma of fresh baked pies, cookies, cakes, and breads. It was heavenly!

The bakery was already quite busy, because today was Saturday and the people were buying their fresh baked pastries and doughnuts for a quick breakfast, and fresh baked bread for the evening meal.

Vikki watched the people deciding and buying, and watched as Mrs. Pellegrino rung up the sales on the register. There were so many delicious goodies; how could anyone decide?

One of Vikki's favorite treats was, of course, the sampling plate. This was a plate on the counter where Mrs. Pellegrino put cookies for her customers to nibble on while they waited. But, as Vikki stood on her tiptoes to look into the plate, it was empty! She tried to get Mrs. Pellegrino's attention to tell her, but she was so busy she just said, "Vikki, honey, take a number. I'll be with you in a minute, sweetie."

Vikki couldn't get Mr. Pellegrino to notice her, either, because he was busy in the back room baking and decorating cakes.

She just knew people would be unhappy if they saw the empty plate, so what do you suppose she did? (You guessed it! That's right). Vikki decided to put her own home-baked cookies on the plate. Wouldn't that make Mrs. Pellegrino and all her customers happy? So, Vikki unwrapped the foil and carefully placed the cookies on the sampling plate for all to enjoy. With that completed, Vikki slipped quietly out the door and off to do another good deed.

But, oh my, what was going on in the bakery as the customers began nibbling on Vikki's cookies? Their noses began to twitch and turn up, their mouths puckered, and their eyes began to water! One by one the people began leaving the bakery - without buying a thing!

To Mrs. Pellegrino's amazement, within a few minutes the bakery was completely empty! "Well, what in the world is going on?" asked Mrs. Pellegrino.

Just about then, Mr. Pellegrino came from the back room and asked, in his Italian accent, "Mama, why you chase'a all the people away?"

Mrs. Pellegrino, almost in tears, replied, "But, Papa, I no chase'a the people away. They leave!"

Vikki was thoroughly satisfied with herself for doing such a good thing for Mr. and Mrs. Pellegrino, and so she just knew that helping Mr. B repair bikes for his customers would make him happy, too! So, off to Mr. B's Bike Shop she went.

But, Mr. B saw Vikki coming, and he quickly pulled his shade and put the "Closed" sign in the window, hoping this would discourage Vikki, and she would go away.

When Vikki saw the shade pulled and the "Closed" sign in the window, she got really worried and set out to see what was wrong with Mr. B. After all, Mr. B never closed his shop; not even the day Vikki accidentally over-greased all the bikes! Even then, Mr. B stayed open all day just to clean them.

Vikki truly loved Mr. B, because he was such a kind and patient man (and when Vikki was around, he needed a lot of patience!). She just couldn't imagine him being sick or something worse; so she decided to visit his home and cheer him up. When she got to his home, he wasn't there!

Oh, no! Now she really began to worry. What if he was being held hostage by a bike burglar in his shop and he was tied up and couldn't call for help? This was definitely a job for the police!

Vikki went down to the police station and explained to the police Captain exactly what happened. (Exactly? Well, maybe not exactly-exactly, but close enough, according to Vikki).

She told the Captain how this big bully of a guy grabbed Mr. B and pushed him into the shop and gagged him and tied him up!

Well, that was all the Captain had to hear. He told Vikki to go home where she would be safe, and he had the dispatcher send a message to the police officers who were out patrolling the town in their police cars.

"Calling all cars, calling all cars. Any police car within the area of Mr. B's Bike Shop go directly there immediately," the dispatcher announced.

Just about the time Mr. B was beginning to re-open his shop again, around the corner of the street came three police cars, with their lights flashing and their sirens howling. They came to a screeching halt in front of Mr. B's Bike Shop. A police officer jumped out of a car and began speaking through a bullhorn, "All right, we've got you surrounded. Come out with your hands up!"

Slowly, the door opened, and out walked a timid Mr. B, with his hands held high over his head.

"Are you okay Mr. B?" asked the officer.

"Ye-yes. I think so," stammered Mr. B.

"Is the burglar still in there?" asked the officer.

"Burglar? What burglar?" asked Mr. B.

After the police officer explained the whole story to him (the way Vikki had told it), Mr. B said, "I'm so shook up after all this, I think I *will* close the shop for the day and go home."

Vikki knew the police would do a good job freeing Mr. B from the burglar, so with another good deed accomplished, off she went in search of someone else to make happy!

This time, Vikki didn't have to go too far to find someone who needed help. Mr. Haile, the barber, was busy sweeping up the hair from his barbershop floor, when Vikki popped in and yelled, "Hello, Mr. Haile! Beautiful day, isn't it?"

"Hello, Vikki. Yes, it is a beautiful day. How are you?" asked Mr. Haile.

"Oh, you know me, Mr. Haile. Always out looking for someone to make happy," replied Vikki.

"That's good, Vikki. Now run along. I have to sweep my shop," answered Mr. Haile.

"What's this?" asked Vikki, as she picked up some poster board and colored markers.

"Oh, those are just some things I'm going to use later to make a sign for my barbershop," answered Mr. Haile.

"I can make a sign for you," said Vikki.

"No, no, that's okay, Vikki. I can do it later, Why don't you just run along, and . . . " Mr. Haile was saying as he was interrupted by the telephone ringing.

"Hello," said Mr. Haile. "Uh-huh, uh-huh, uh-huh," he was saying to the person on the phone.

While he was busy talking and laughing on the phone, Vikki decided to make a sign for his shop.

"Let's see. What would make the people happy to come in and get a haircut?" thought Vikki. She suddenly remembered her dad saying how he needed a haircut, but didn't have enough money to get one right now.

"I know," thought Vikki, "the sign I make will allow everyone to come in and get a haircut."

So, after Vikki finished making the sign with big bold black letters, and decorating it with cute little heads (some of them slightly bald, like her daddy's head), the sign read, "FREE HAIRCUTS -- ALL DAY LONG."

Vikki put the sign in the window while Mr. Haile was busy talking on the phone. He didn't see the sign, or see Vikki put the sign in the window, but Vikki just knew he would be happy when he saw the sign later.

She left the barbershop, just as it began to rain (didn't Vikki tell you it was going to rain?)

Vikki was so happy it was raining. She just loved the rain. After raining for awhile, little puddles began forming on the ground. This was Vikki's favorite thing about the rain – the puddles!

She began jumping from one puddle to the next, trying to splash the water out of them. (Well, they didn't all have just rainwater in them – some of them had mud!)

In no time at all, Vikki had splashed gooey brown mud all over her pretty yellow rain boots, and her pretty yellow raincoat, and her pretty yellow rain hat (and yes, even her pretty rose-colored glasses).

"Uh-oh," said Vikki, "I'm a mess! How am I going to get this stuff off of me? Oh, I know. I'll go down to Fountain's Car Wash." So off she skipped to get cleaned up.

When she got to the car wash, Mr. Clark, the owner, told her to sit in the waiting room so she wouldn't get hurt.

"Get hurt?" asked Vikki. "How can I get hurt in a car wash? It's just water!"

"Okay, Vikki, but please stay out of the way," said Mr. Clark.

When Mr. Clark wasn't looking, Vikki crawled into a nice red car that was getting ready to go through the car wash. She didn't pick just any old car. She picked one that could help her get clean. She picked this one, because, well, because it had a top that opened up. It was a convertible.

Vikki pushed a button, and the top of the car began folding down. As the car went through the car wash, Vikki yelled, "Weee! This is fun," and the water and soapsuds covered her all over (including the inside of the beautiful red convertible!)

"Oh, how nice," said Vikki, "This man's car is getting cleaned on the inside as well as the outside. Won't he be happy?" After it stopped, she climbed out of the car, and as she walked, her little yellow rain boots sloshed and squeaked with each step she took. (They were full of water, but Vikki was happy, and she just knew Mr. Clark would be happy that she helped him clean the beautiful red car). Vikki trotted off down the street, looking for another person to make happy in the town of New Ipswich.

She walked around for a long time, but couldn't find anyone who needed to be helped. Everyone she met seemed to be happy, or didn't need any help, so she decided she had better go home and see what her mom had made for dinner.

When Vikki got to her house, she could see through the window that there were a lot of people in her house. Maybe her mom and dad were having a party for her! Oh, boy! Vikki couldn't wait to get inside and join the party!

As soon as she got near the door, she could hear everyone talking at once with what sounded like loud, angry voices. She couldn't imagine a party where everyone sounded angry with one another, but she had to go inside and find out what was going on.

When she opened the door, everyone stopped talking and looked at her. Right there, standing in her living room, were Mr. and Mrs. Pellegrino; Mr. B; the police Captain and a few police officers; Mr. Haile and some of his customers; Mr. Clark, and yes - even the owner of the beautiful red, thoroughly soaked convertible. Are they here to thank me, she wondered?

Well, they weren't exactly there to thank her, and this wasn't exactly a party, and Vikki wasn't exactly sure everyone was happy to see her, either!

Vikki's dad motioned for her to come in a little closer so that everyone could talk to her, and explain to her why they had come to visit.

Mr. and Mrs. Pellegrino told her that they didn't have another customer for the rest of the day. Upon cleaning up the bakery, they happened to nibble on the cookies left in the sampling plate, and figured out why all the people had left the bakery. The cookies were very salty, and very, very bitter.

Mr. B was so nervous after being frightened by the police at his shop, that he had to lie down several hours with a cold washcloth on his forehead.

The police Captain and the police officers explained to Vikki how serious and dangerous it was to file a false report with the police department. They told her she should make sure she tells them exactly what happened if she sees something wrong; and not just make up a story that she thinks is true.

Then Mr. Haile explained that he had five people come into his barbershop at one time for a haircut. After he finished with one customer, the man got up and said, "Thanks a lot for the free haircut, Mr. Haile. That was awfully kind of you. See you later," and left without paying.

Surprised at the customer, Mr. Haile questioned the other customers who were waiting, and finally discovered the sign in his window.

Mr. Clark explained the mess Vikki had caused to his customer's car. Vikki said she was sorry to Mr. Clark and his customer.

"That's okay," said the customer, "Mr. Clark got all the water out, and now it's at home drying."

After everyone had a chance to talk to Vikki about what she had done to them, she told them she didn't realize she had made them so unhappy. She was only trying to do good deeds and make everyone happy. What a mess she had caused!

She told them all she was very sorry, and that she would never do those things again. Everyone forgave her, and her mom and dad thanked everyone for being so understanding.

Mr. B said, "Now, I am happy."

Everyone else said the same thing, and they all left with smiles on their faces.

"See, Dad," said Vikki, "I made everyone happy today after all!" And, with that, Vikki began walking out the door.

"Vikki, where are you going now?" asked Dad.

"I'm going to Mrs. Hendrick's house to transplant her geraniums for her," replied Vikki.

"Wait just a minute, young lady," her dad said. "If you really want to make someone happy, go in the kitchen with your mom and help her clean up the mess you made today."

"Oh, all right," replied Vikki, "I guess helping Mom clean up would make her happy." So, off she skipped to pick up, clean, scrub, and put away everything she had left out this morning.

When Vikki was completely through with the mess, her mom told her to go out and play until dinner (because she was very happy with her work). Vikki went in the living room to ask Dad if it was okay for her to transplant Mrs. Hendrick's geraniums now.

"Okay," said Dad, "just stay out of trouble."

Well, Vikki didn't exactly tell Mrs. Hendricks she would transplant her geraniums for her. And, Mrs. Hendricks didn't exactly ask her to transplant them. But, Vikki just knew Mrs. Hendricks would be happy if she saw her window box geraniums planted all over her front yard where they would have much more room to grow and breathe. (After all, wouldn't the geraniums be happy?)

- - - - - - - THE END - - - - - - -

Printed in the United States
by Baker & Taylor Publisher Services